My Brother's a Keeper

This edition published 2008
First published 2000 by
A & C Black Publishers Ltd
38 Soho Square, London, W1D 3HB

www.acblack.com

Text copyright © 2000 Michael Hardcastle
Illustrations copyright © 2000 Bob Moulder
Cover illustration copyright © 2008 Anthony Williams

The rights of Michael Hardcastle and Bob Moulder to be
identified as author and illustrator of this work respectively
have been asserted by them in accordance with the
Copyrights, Designs and Patents Act 1988.

ISBN 978-0-7136-8628-9

A CIP catalogue for this book is available
from the British Library.

This book is produced using paper that is made from wood
grown in managed, sustainable forests. It is natural, renewable and
recyclable. The logging and manufacturing processes conform to
the environmental regulations of the country of origin.

Printed and bound in China by C&C Offset Printing.

**Essex County
Council Libraries**

My Brother's a Keeper

Michael Hardcastle

illustrated by Bob Moulder

A & C Black • London

CHAPTER ONE

What are we going to do?

Gavin, the coach, was in despair.

We need another keeper. That injury of Tommy's is going to keep him out for weeks.

Alex, the skipper, looked at his team sprawled on the benches in the changing room.

Pete could take over. You play a good game of basketball, don't you, Pete? You can catch a ball.

The coach shook his head.

No, no, we need someone with experience. You can't have just anybody in front of the goal. We need a real keeper. Otherwise we'll leak goals like a sink without a plug.

7

8

Alex spoke in a serious voice.

Well, I hope he can help us out. Tommy's broken hand will take weeks to heal. If we don't get a decent keeper, I think the *coach* might quit.

He always says he only wants to work with winners. He might leave if we have a bad season.

Carlo was still thinking about that when he reached home.

13

His mum was always saying that. Usually, Carlo ignored it. Now it seemed like a good idea because he could see if Justin was any good as a keeper. To his surprise, he found himself wishing that Justin was the best. Then the coach would be sure to stay with the Raiders, Carlo's team.

If he's got a ball with him, it must be mine. He doesn't have one of his own.

The football pitches were at the far end of Green Park, a kind of hollow surrounded by trees and bushes. It was a favorite spot for dog walkers.

A man in a tracksuit stood there. With him was a big dog. Suddenly, a ball bounced in front of the man.

The man walked off, grinning.

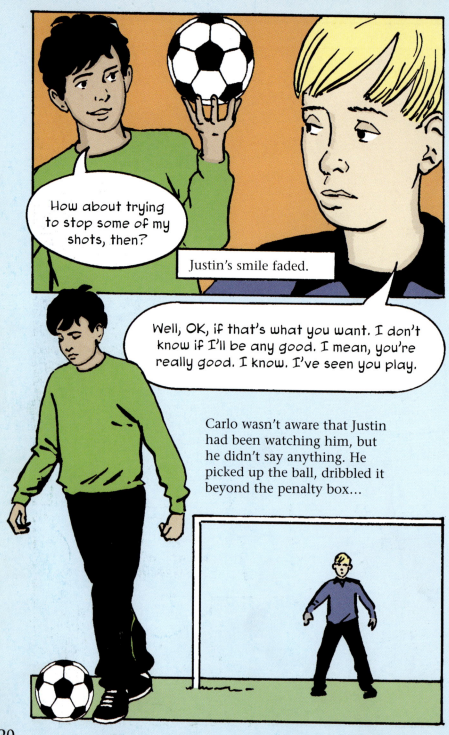

How about trying to stop some of my shots, then?

Justin's smile faded.

Well, OK, if that's what you want. I don't know if I'll be any good. I mean, you're really good. I know. I've seen you play.

Carlo wasn't aware that Justin had been watching him, but he didn't say anything. He picked up the ball, dribbled it beyond the penalty box...

In the next few minutes,
however, Justin saved very little.

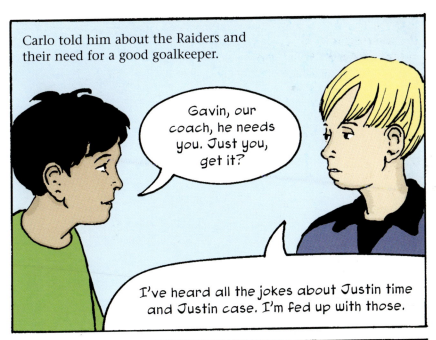

Carlo told him about the Raiders and their need for a good goalkeeper.

Gavin, our coach, he needs you. Just you, get it?

I've heard all the jokes about Justin time and Justin case. I'm fed up with those.

Sorry. I won't do it again. Listen, come to training on Tuesday. Then Gavin can make up his own mind.

Maybe.

Justin didn't seem very interested. A few minutes later, he said he was tired and wanted to go home.

Mrs Hart was pleased to see them coming home together.

Did you have a good game?

Didn't play a game. We just fooled around.

Justin gave Carlo a strange look but didn't say anything.

Carlo nodded. He knew that Justin and his mum
enjoyed swimming much more than he did, but he
thought it was a good idea to go along with them.

CHAPTER TWO

The pool was crowded and Carlo was tired of swimming.
His mum and Justin had been racing each other.
Justin had strong shoulders and a powerful stroke.
Usually, he won, but only just. Carlo watched them
climb out of the water. They were just about as tall
as each other. He felt a sudden stab of jealousy.

Want some help, Carlo?

I can manage.

Justin looked surprised but he managed to hide how hurt he felt.

Sorry. No offence.

Carlo nodded. During the next few minutes, as they all changed into their clothes, Carlo kept thinking about how things were changing at home. His own dad had left. Now he had a new one, Justin's father, though he worked away from home most of the time.

He was fairly sure his mum would stay the same with him, but she was definitely fussing over Justin, always joking with him and offering him extra helpings at meals.

To be fair Justin usually said that he didn't want any special treatment just because he was new to the family.

Justin's dad didn't try to be extra friendly with Carlo. He was sort of neutral, like a referee. But Carlo wondered if his relationship with his mum would suffer now that she had two other people to care for all the time.

Carlo and his mum were waiting for Justin to join them.

Justin really likes you, Mum, doesn't he?

I'm glad he does.

After all, he doesn't have a mum of his own now, does he?

CHAPTER THREE

Gavin nodded with approval when he met Justin.

Well, you're built like a goalie, tall and broad. Have you played for a team before?

Only when I was little. My dad and I moved around a lot so I never joined a real team. My dad used to be in the Army.

Then we'll just have to see how you are tonight, son. We'll give you the full treatment: shots, corners, free kicks and scrambles.

Let's see how you do.

Carlo saw Justin bite his lip. His stepbrother looked really nervous. Carlo didn't know why he should feel that way because he remembered Justin's amazing save from the dog man. And there had been talk of other "great" saves.

Pete stood in front of Justin when they practised corner kicks. Pete was the tallest defender in the Raiders' squad and scored plenty of goals from set pieces. He he'd been told by Gavin to give Justin a hard time to test him out.

The ball came over...

Justin caught it, but...

AHHH!

Justin turned pink.

Sorry.

Gavin frowned.

Well, son, don't do it again. First rule of keeping: catch the ball and stick to it.

Justin improved on that first fumble.

But he rarely looked confident whatever he was doing.

Carlo fired in a couple of fierce shots and was glad when his stepbrother tipped one over the bar.

Gavin was pleased, too.

OOOF!

That's the way to do it, son. Keep watching the ball.

When the coach said it was time for a break, most of the players flopped down on the grass. Alex handed out soft drinks and energy bars that his dad always supplied for the team. Then Gavin and Alex went into a huddle for some private talk.

So what happens if a scout comes along to watch you? I mean, top teams could be interested in any of us if we have a good season. And I've seen you when you're really good.

Justin gave him a grateful glance.

Thanks for trying to make me feel better, Carlo. That helps, it really does.

But, well, if a scout turns up, I'll have to hope I don't notice him watching me. Trouble is, when you're in goal you often have the chance to look around and see who's there. Sometimes you catch people staring at you as if nobody else existed. That's — well — weird.

Yeah, I see what you mean. Doesn't bother me whether I'm being watched or not. But I suppose we're all different.

Justin improved during the second part of the training session, but he still didn't look happy.

Good save, mate!

At the end of the session, Gavin had made up his mind. He took Justin to one side.

Look, I'd like you to play for us in the Cup-tie against the Chargers. But you need to work on your catching before then. Get some practice in with that brother of yours.

I will. I've always hated practice. I'm better in a real match.

Make sure you are. I don't have anyone else to play in goal and we want to win this Cup.

CHAPTER FOUR

The following day, Carlo burst into the sitting room.

Justin, I've fixed up a five-a-side game. Right now. In Green Park. So, come on!

Well, I'm not sure.

Justin looked up at his stepmother.

Go on, Justin. We can finish this another time.

You shouldn't miss the chance of playing some football with Carlo.

OK.

I'll go and change into my kit. Won't be a minute.

Is this game just for Justin's benefit?

Not really. It'll be good for all of us with the Cup-tie so close. But, yeah, the extra practice will be good for him, Alex says. He's our skipper, you know.

Of course I know. I've always followed your games. And now I've got both my boys in the team!

Since most of the players were from the Raiders' squad, Alex had decided their defenders should be on one side and the attackers on the other.

Gives us a chance to really test each other out.

Nobody argued because they were all eager to win the Cup. Carlo grinned at his stepbrother.

I'll put a hat-trick past you!

Just try it. I'll stop every shot that comes my way.

In fact, the defenders defended so well that Justin didn't have a shot of any kind to save for quite a long time. Alex was in terrific form, snuffing out any move that threatened danger, and then setting up attacks of his own.

Justin was a spectator until a team-mate turned the ball back to him so that he could get into the game. He was beginning to wish Alex would make a mistake or two just so he could practise catching and diving and kicking.

49

Then, as the defenders pushed further and further upfield, the ball suddenly got loose. Carlo darted past everyone to reach it.

Only Justin could stop the goal. He didn't hesitate.

As Carlo set up to shoot, Justin dived.

Alex rushed up to Justin.

Great keeping! You really saved us there!

Thanks, but I've hurt my leg, and I think Carlo is hurt, too.

Neither of the stepbrothers could keep playing, so Alex called the game off.

We'd better get you guys home. At least you live in the same house!

Luckily, they didn't have far to go. The other players gave them a hand and even cracked a few jokes.

Goalies aren't supposed to get leg injuries, are they?

Justin liked his new team-mates so he tried to grin, but his leg hurt too much.

53

See you Sunday. Make sure you're fit by then.

Mrs Hart looked worried as both boys limped into the house.

What on earth happened to you?

I kicked him. And I hurt myself at the same time.

It was an accident. Carlo didn't mean to.

Right, I'd better see what needs doing. Looks like you'll have a nasty bruise on your thigh, Justin. But if we get some ice on it quickly you won't suffer too much, I hope. I'll try to be very gentle!

Carlo didn't mind his mum attending to Justin first. After all, he'd not only caused the injury but his plan to give Justin some extra practice had back-fired. By now his own injury was less painful. With luck, he'd avoid the ice treatment altogether.

Justin didn't complain even once about the discomfort he experienced that evening. At bedtime, when Carlo tried to apologise again for the collision, his stepbrother just grinned.

Your mum told me we're getting to be more like twins every day. I think she's right! But don't expect me to score the goals on Sunday, brother.

I promise I'll do my best. Listen, Mum said she might drop by to watch for a bit. Will you be able to cope? She doesn't want to miss our first big match together.

That's fine, Carlo. She'll be watching you.

This time, Justin actually seemed pleased at the thought of being watched.

As the home side, the Chargers were expected to attack from the kick-off, and they did. Their yellow-shirted forwards were all strong, hard runners who really lived up to the team's name.

59

Within a minute, Justin was in action, coming out to catch a high cross aimed at the centre forward.

AAGH!

He took the ball cleanly and confidently.

To his surprise, he saw that Gavin was applauding him.

That's it son! First rule: catch the ball and stick to it.

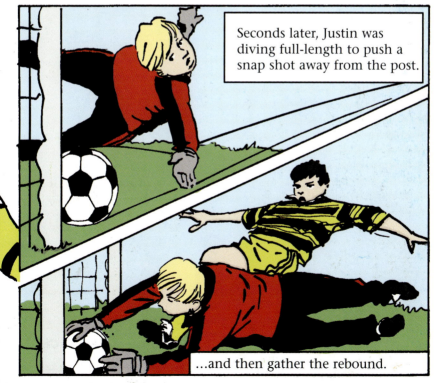

Seconds later, Justin was diving full-length to push a snap shot away from the post.

...and then gather the rebound.

That kick was wasted.
But a few moments
later the ball ran loose.

Justin didn't get hold of it at first, and then suddenly
it was thudding into his chest from a fierce kick.

Thankfully, he held on to it before
clearing the danger with a long kick.

Gavin was talking to one of the subs.

That goalie of ours is like some actors.

Dreadful at rehearsals. But brilliant when they have to peform for real.

Of course, Justin couldn't hear that neat comparison but soon he had something to smile about.

Justin spotted Mrs Hart in the crowd, but he didn't
want to wave in case the coach disapproved.

He just hoped they'd still play well.

With the Chargers still attacking, Alex pulled off a great tackle.

Then he set off on a run with the ball.

Everyone seemed to expect him to pass, but he kept going.

Carlo yelled at him from just outside the box.

Mine!

Alex gave him the ball with an inch-perfect pass.

SWOOSH!

Carlo turned...

...jinked past one defender.

Gavin talked to his team.

Well done, boys, you're on your way to winning this.

So don't let it slip. Great stuff, you brothers. Keep shining like stars!

Carlo and Justin exchanged grins.

The Raiders' lead didn't last long when the game resumed. Once again the Chargers attacked fiercely. Pete was right on the edge of the box when he brought down one of their strikers. Only the Chargers' players and the referee thought it was a bad enough foul for a penalty.

Justin groaned when he knew he had to face a spot-kick.

Almost at once, the Chargers were back on the attack. Justin had to fist the ball clear from one raid...

...and then smother another shot on the line. He was determined that the ball wouldn't pass him again.

Gradually the Chargers tired. Their attacks fell apart. With time running out, the score was still 1–1 and a replay was likely.

Justin was surprised at how far his kick went.

Alex, near the half-way line, simply lobbed it on when it reached him.

Once again it went to Carlo, who wasn't defended because he'd been out of the game for so long.

Justin watched eagerly as Carlo took the ball on for just a few metres.

Then Carlo saw that the Charger goalie was on the edge of his box. The goal was unguarded! Carlo took aim and hit the ball hard and high.

Desperately, the goalie tried to
back-pedal, but he was too late.

The ball passed over
his head, dipped, and
landed in the net.

78

All the Raiders and their fans yelled. Mrs Hart was dancing up and down. Gavin was punching the air. Even the Charger fans knew the winning goal had just been scored.

Two minutes later, the final whistle sounded.

A spectator congratulated Carlo as the players began to leave the field.

Great goal!

But that goalie really made the second one for you. Who is he?

Oh, my brother's the keeper.

Terrific, isn't he?